Mr. Bear's Adventure

Linda Garcia

Illustrated by Diana Boles

First Edition

NEWMAN SPRINGS PUBLISHING
320 Broad Street
Red Bank, NJ 07701

First originally published by Newman Springs Publishing 2021

ISBN 978-1-63692-438-0 (Paperback)
ISBN 978-1-63692-439-7 (Digital)

Printed in the United States of America

To my parents, Ruth and Bucky Jenkins, for all their love and support, always.

It was a beautiful, sunny morning, and Mr. Bear thought it was the perfect day for an adventure.

So he got busy filling his rucksack with a picnic lunch filled with berries, nuts, corn, and honey.

He then headed out toward the edge of town, where the four corners meet.

This is where he would start his adventure.

Mr. Bear is so excited for the day that he nearly tripped on a rock.

“Hey, watch it!” yelled the rock.

Which wasn’t a rock at all! Suddenly a small head peered out from under what he had thought was a rock.

“Hello,” said Mr. Bear to the little rock.

A little voice from inside the rock said “hello” in return.

“Oh my!” said Mr. Bear. “Who are you?” he asked.

“I’m Teddy Turtle, and I live in my shell. Who are you?” he asked.

“I’m Mr. Bear,” he said, “and I live in a cave just outside of town.”

"I'm on an adventure today, would you like to join me?"

Teddy looked down, kind of sad, and replied, "I walk very slowly and would only hold you up."

Teddy then thanked Mr. Bear for inviting him and told him, if he wanted to stop by on his way back home, he would love to hear all about his adventure.

Mr. Bear thought that was a great idea and headed back down the dirt road. He was so happy to have made a new friend.

This is going to be a great adventure, he thought to himself.

As he walked along kicking a pebble, he thought about the new friend he had met.

He continued walking down the road, enjoying the day, when all of a sudden he heard a rustling noise coming from the bushes just up ahead.

What could that be? he wondered.

Right across the road just behind the bushes, he saw a large bird, bigger than any bird he had ever seen before!

"Hello," he said. "I'm Mr. Bear, who are you?"

"I'm Tommy Turkey," he replied. "Where are you heading on this perfectly wonderful day?"

"I'm on an adventure, would you like to join me?"

“Oh, that sounds like fun,” said Tommy. “I believe I would like that very much.”

So the two of them headed back down the road together.

As they were walking toward the waterfall, they heard a scratching noise behind the bushes.

All of a sudden, a furry little brown animal hopped out in front of them.

"Hi! I'm Roxy Rabbit. Who are you?" she asked.

"I'm Mr. Bear, and this is Tommy Turkey. And we are on an adventure today.

"Would you like to join us?" they asked.

"Oh my! I would love to go on an adventure with you," she said, and the three of them headed back down the road.

They were looking for the perfect place to have a picnic when just past the waterfall they saw a beautiful clearing.

“This is the perfect place for a picnic.” said Mr. Bear.

As they were setting up the picnic of berries, nuts, corn, and honey along with clover they had picked for Roxy, they heard something coming from a tall tree at the edge of the clearing.

The three of them followed the noise up the tree to a large branch.

“Up there!” they all shouted.

A big gray and black animal was sitting on the branch, looking down at them.

Mr. Bear said, "Hello, we are having a picnic, would you care to join us?"

The animal shouted back, "Yes, I would like that very much!" He climbed down the tree quickly. "Hi! I'm Ricky Raccoon," he said. "Who might you be?"

They each introduced themselves to Ricky before explaining about their adventure. "I'm Mr. Bear, and this is Tommy Turkey and Roxy Rabbit. We are on an adventure today and stopped to have a picnic.

“You are welcome to join our adventure after lunch, if you’d like.”

Ricky Raccoon replied that he would like that, indeed.

They all sat down and enjoyed their picnic lunch of berries, nuts, corn, honey, and clover.

"Hey, Mr. Bear, do you know what is on the other side of this clearing?" asked Tommy Turkey.

"Actually, I do. My dear friend, Mr. Buck, lives there."

"Mr. Buck is the oldest deer in the forest and a good friend of mine," said Mr. Bear. "Would you like to meet him?" he asked.

"Oh yes," they all replied, and on they went to Mr. Buck's house just on the other side of the clearing.

When they arrived, they were all so excited to share their adventure with Mr. Buck that they were all talking at once.

"Hold on there, little ones. I can't hear you if you all talk at once."

They slowed down and began to tell him all about the adventure they were on.

Mr. Buck was smiling when they were all done. "Wow! That has been quite an adventure indeed," he said. And he wished he could join them, but he was way too busy today. Maybe next time.

So they said their goodbyes to Mr. Buck and headed back to their picnic, which they hadn't finished eating.

Once they finished their picnic, they packed everything up and headed back out on their adventure.

The four new friends headed back down the road and, before long, were standing in front of a beautiful pond.

"This is a nice spot to go fishing," said Mr. Bear. "Maybe we could all go fishing here some time."

They all agreed that was a fabulous idea. Then once again, down the road they went.

Tommy was the first to admit he was getting tired.

They all soon agreed that it had been the best adventure, especially meeting each other and Mr. Buck.

Mr. Bear agreed; it had been a great adventure, but yes, it was time to head home.

Mr. Bear thanked each of his new friends for joining his adventure and promised to plan a fishing one soon.

They said their goodbyes, and each headed on their way, saying, "Until next time when we go fishing!"

Mr. Bear, being true to his word, did stop by to tell Teddy Turtle all about the adventure and the new friends he had made along the way.

Teddy was so happy to hear all about it and said he would like to meet all these new friends one day and go fishing.

Mr. Bear said that sounded like a great plan.

Saying goodbye, he headed home, as well.

What a wonderful adventure it had been on this perfectly wonderful day!

About the Author

If you can dream it, you can create it. I always wanted to write, and although it took me a very long time to actually submit my stories for print, the journey was totally worth the wait. A girl, now a Nana begins her first children's book series shortly before retiring. A dream come true.

CPSIA information can be obtained
at www.ICGtesting.com
Printed in the USA
LVHW070236281221
707328LV00007B/46